For Alyssa—J.J.

To Mom—P.O.

The Big Cheese
Text copyright © 2023 by Jory John
Illustrations copyright © 2023 by Pete Oswald
All rights reserved. Manufactured in Italy.
No part of this book may be used or reproduced in any manner whatsoever
without written permission except in the case of brief quotations
embodied in critical articles and reviews.
For information address HarperCollins Children's Books,
a division of HarperCollins Publishers, 195 Broadway, New York, NY 10007.
www.harpercollinschildrens.com

Library of Congress Control Number: 2023933846
ISBN 978-0-06-332950-8 (trade bdg.) — ISBN 978-0-06-335517-0 (special ed.)
ISBN 978-0-06-335269-8 (intl. ed.)

The artist used scanned watercolor textures
and digital paint to create the illustrations for this book.
23 24 25 26 27 RTLO 10 9 8 7 6 5 4 3 2 1

First Edition

THE BIG CHEESE

written by **JORY JOHN**

illustrated by **PETE OSWALD**

HARPER

An Imprint of HarperCollinsPublishers

That's right, folks. I'm the biggest, cheesiest piece of cheddar around.

I'm really something to behold.
Take a good look at me.
Are you seeing what I'm seeing? *Hmm?!*
Have you EVER observed a more
impressive cheese in your life?

It's not just my stature, either. It's my presence. My vibe.
The energy I emanate. The excitement I exude.

It's the way I fill a room,

or a theater,

or a stadium.

Wherever I go, I cause a fuss.
Heads turn. Jaws drop. Gasps are audible.
That's why they call me Cheese.

Oh, say it with me, please . . .
THE BIG CHEESE!

"TA-DA."

YOU'D BETTER BELIEVE IT.

How did I get such a good—or should I say *gouda*—reputation?

Well . . . I wasn't always a big shot.
I grew up on a crowded platter in a tiny kitchen.
I was an unremarkable little curd. We lived quiet lives
of pasteurization.

But I wasn't happy with the status quo, oh no.
I wanted to make a big ol' name for myself.
So I resolved to become a Big Cheese.

I wanted the praise. The cheers. The spotlight. The attention. The ovations. The celebrations.
I set to work and, before long, I was on the fast track to success.

I dressed to impress.

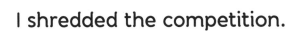

I shredded the competition.

I stole every show.

And then I'd brag nonstop to anybody who'd listen.

What was the secret to my success?
Well, I stuck to the things I was good at.
That way, I couldn't *possibly* fail.

Did it get a little boring never trying anything new?
I suppose.
But it didn't matter as long as everyone agreed that I was . . .

oh, say it with me, please . . .
THE BIG CHEESE!

"TA-DA."

But then, one fateful day, I met Wedge.
He was new in town and he seemed to be
my exact *opposite* in every way.

He was
quiet.

I was loud.

He was shy.

I was bold.

While I dominated conversations, he kept to himself.

I didn't pay him much attention at first, because why would I?
I was too preoccupied with being the center of *my* universe.

But then, without warning, everything changed.

Here's what happened:

Every summer, our tiny village staged an all-day Cheese-cathlon. Guess who had first-place trophies from the last six years? Hmm?

This year's opening ceremony started at 5 a.m., *sharp*.
I was fully primed and prepared to prevail.

First up was a footrace, and I zipped into the lead.

Within seconds, though, there was someone on my heels.
I could hear his breath, the pitter-patter of his agile feet.
It was Wedge!

I. COULD. NOT. BELIEVE IT!

Oh, he was fast.
Not just fast, but skilled. Disciplined. He paced himself.
We were neck and neck for most of the race, but
when I slipped on a rogue pebble . . .

Wedge swerved, sped up,
and beat me by a nose.
A *cheese*-nose!

For the first time, I'd come in *second* place.
Oh, the indignity!
But there was no time to sulk because the *next* leg
of the competition had already started.

It was a game of chess.

Before I could blink or think, Wedge had taken my king
in four moves and—while I was busy protesting to the
judges—he'd already moved on.

The following events were a blur of loss
after loss after humiliating loss.

It turned out that Wedge was quietly excellent at . . . *everything*.
Even when he won, though, he didn't gloat.
He was *sooooo* humble.

It was . . . odd.

It was . . . disconcerting.

It was . . . absolutely BAFFLING!

Finally, I watched in dismay as Wedge trounced
me one last time, and the day came to a bitter end.

Well . . . bitter for *me*, at least. I went
through every possible emotion . . .

until I'd finally exhausted myself.

And as I lay in the muck, I heard a thunderous voice making the dreaded announcement:

The crowd roared its approval.

What had just happened?!
It was honestly hard to fathom.

"HMM."

I closed my eyes.
Suddenly . . . inexplicably . . .
I felt a sense of calm come over me.
I listened to my breathing, to the steady beating of my heart.

Yes, I had lost. Again and again and *again.*
But after all that, I actually felt . . . okay. *Relieved,* even.
I suddenly knew that my world wasn't going to crumble.

I picked myself up. I dusted myself off. And I headed home.

Before too long, I spotted Wedge.
He wasn't busy celebrating or bragging.
He was just watching the stream go by.
He looked content.

We chatted for a bit.
It turned out that Wedge had a fascinating life story.
I found myself getting caught up in a great conversation.
A conversation that wasn't all about *me*.
Huh.

That day, I realized something: Maybe it didn't matter
if I wasn't the best at everything.
In fact, perhaps it was *healthy* for me to lose for once.

And sure, my ego was bruised in the short term.
But over time, I gained some perspective on what's *really* important.

Losing taught me about empathy and humility.

GO, TEAM!

It showed me that I'd become so focused on *winning* that I was missing out on the joy of *participating.*

And it helped me see that I can live with defeat . . . *even* if I get a bit angry or frustrated at first.

These days, I'm trying not to worry about whether I win or lose.

I don't have to impress everyone all the time. I let *others* have the spotlight.

And I've taken up some new hobbies . . . just for *me*.

Yes, I'm trying to be a better wheel of cheddar.
So now, when I brag about something, well . . .
I mostly brag about my *friends*.

Because it turns out that anyone—from a crumb of Gorgonzola to a fleck of feta to an unassuming wedge of Brie—can be . . .